To my grandmother Kanakavalli
who always believed her glass was half-full.
– Chitra Soundar

Farmer Falgu Goes to the Market

Chitra Soundar

Kanika Nair

It was market day.
Farmer Falgu loaded his cart with
baskets of tomatoes,
sacks of onions,
bags of green chilies,
bunches of cilantro,
white eggs,
brown eggs,
and some duck eggs too.

And then, he set off to the
market!

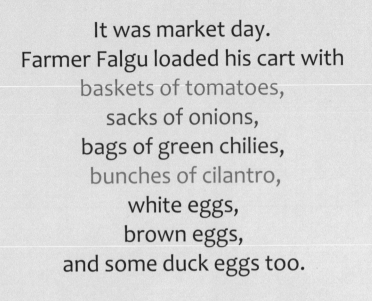

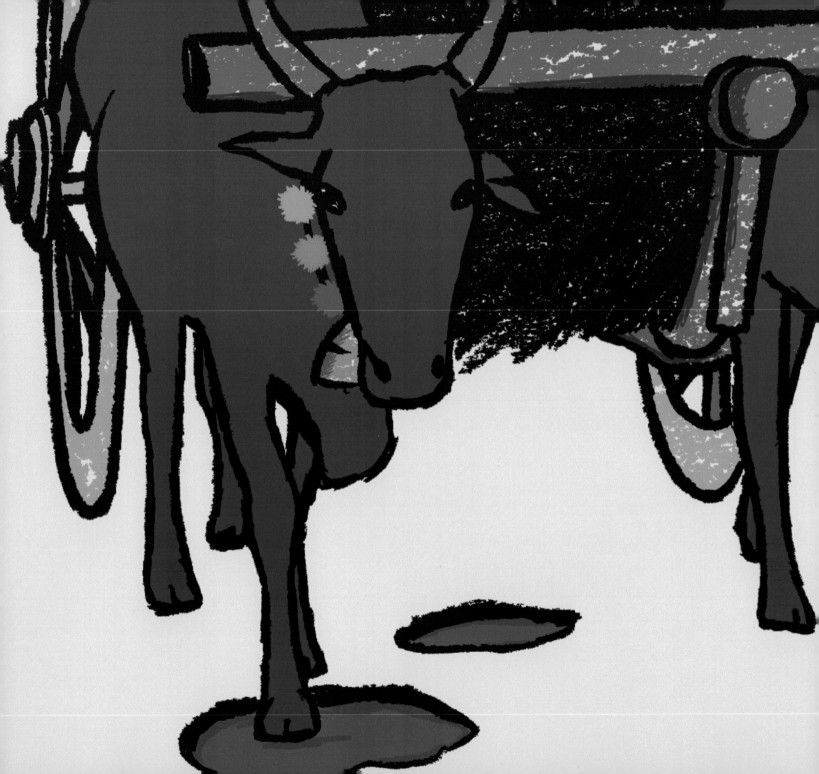

The oxen happily trotted down the road:

trot-trot-trot.

The road had potholes.

Bump! Dunk!

The cart wobbled and rattled.

"Stop! Stop!"

shouted Farmer Falgu.

He turned and inspected his vegetables.
The tomatoes were fine.
The cilantro looked comfortable.
But what was that?

"Oh no!" he cried.

The white eggs were cracked.

He examined the other baskets.
Luckily, the brown eggs and
the duck eggs were intact.

Farmer Falgu set off again:
trot-trot-trot.

A family of ducks crossed the road:
quack-quack!

"Whoa!"
shouted Farmer Falgu.
"Watch where you are going!"

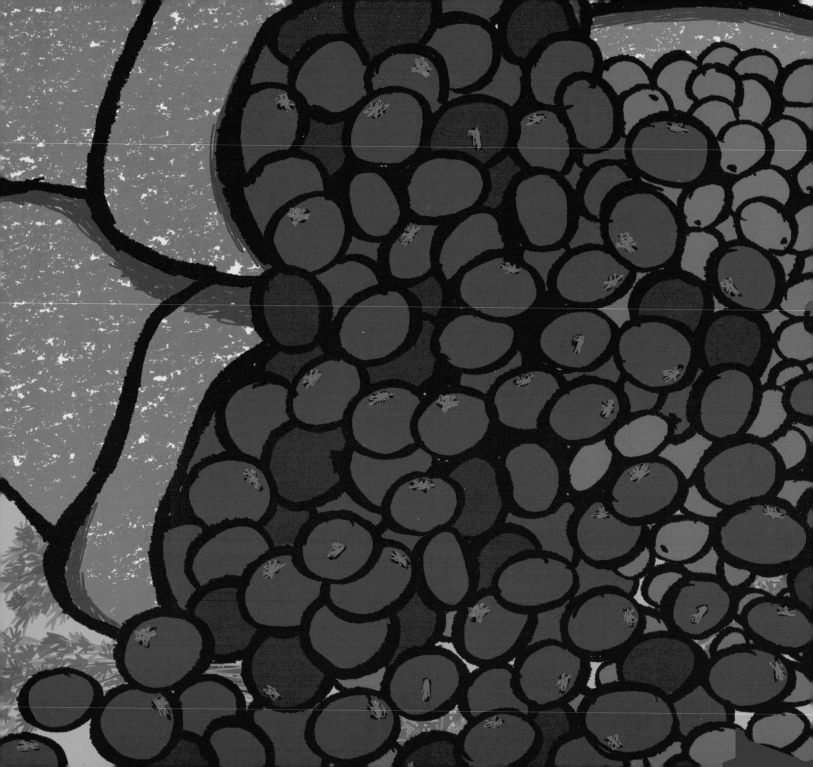

But Mama Duck and little ducks waddled along slowly.

The oxen stopped.
The cart rattled.
The baskets toppled.
The sacks slid down from their perch.
Bags of green chilies and bunches of cilantro
were squashed under the onions.

Farmer Falgu jumped to catch the brown eggs
as they slid down from their perch.

"Oh no!"

he despaired.
Now the brown eggs were
cracked too.

The market was still a few miles away.
Farmer Falgu looked at his cart.
"Well," he thought. "I still have
the baskets of tomatoes,
the sacks of onions,
the bags of green chilies,
and many bunches of cilantro.
And, I have the duck eggs too!"

"Go slow,"

he told his oxen as he got back on to the cart.
He picked up the basket of duck eggs
and placed it on his lap.

The cart went past a family of goats.
The cart went past a crowd of children.
Farmer Falgu checked the eggs.
Everything was fine.

Until...

A big truck sped past the
ox-cart, blaring

honk-honk!

The oxen veered down the road.
Farmer Falgu was thrown against the side.

The duck eggs fell on top of the onions.

Thud!

"Oh no!"

wailed Farmer Falgu.
The duck eggs were
cracked too.

Now all the eggs were cracked,
the cilantro was squashed,
the green chilies crushed.
Farmer Falgu wondered if he should go back home.

"No, I'll go and try my best," he decided.
"The market is not far away."

But as soon as he reached the market...

Maa-maa!

The goats tried to eat his cilantro.

Oink-oink!

The pigs splashed mud over the cart!

Farmer Falgu looked around.
There was only one thing to do.

He found his friend Kishan.
"Kishan!" he called out. "Do you
have a pan I can borrow?"

Farmer Falgu fetched a pan from
Kishan's shop.
He lit up the stove,
sliced the onions,
diced the tomatoes,
and chopped the green chilies.
The pan
sizzled
on the stove.

Crack! Farmer Falgu broke the cracked eggs and stirred.
The eggs bubbled. The smell wafted through the market.

And quickly,
a long line formed
to eat Farmer Falgu's
delicious omelets!

CHITRA SOUNDAR

Chitra hails from India, resides in London, and lives in imaginary worlds woven out of stories. She has written over twenty books for children, ages 3 - 10. Chitra also loves to retell folktales, legends, and ancient tales from the Indian sub-continent. Though she dabbles in chapter books, her first love is picture books.

KANIKA NAIR

Kanika has always had a passion for illustration. After receiving a bachelor's degree in Communication Design from Pearl Academy of Fashion, New Delhi, she began working as a freelance illustrator, writer, and designer of children's books. She loves to incorporate various insights about children that she has collected over the years in her illustrations. The Indian cultural canvas has always fascinated her, which is evident in her artistic style.

Farmer Falgu Goes to the Market

Text copyright © 2014 Chitra Soundar.
Illustration copyright © 2014 Karadi Tales Company Pvt. Ltd.

First U.S. Print 2018

Text: Chitra Soundar
Illustrations: Kanika Nair

Karadi Tales Company Pvt. Ltd.
3A, Dev Regency, 11, First Main Road,
Gandhinagar, Adyar, Chennai 600 020
Tel: +91 44 4205 4243
email: contact@karaditales.com
Website: www.karaditales.com

Printed at: Mentor Printing and Logistics Pvt. Ltd., India

Cataloging - in - Publication information:

Chitra Soundar
Farmer Falgu Goes to the Market / Chitra Soundar;
Illustrated by Kanika Nair
p.32; color illustrations; 23 x 20.5 cm.

1. Travel--Juvenile literature. 2. Conduct of life--Humor.
3. Conduct of life--Juvenile fiction.

PZ7   [E]

JUV001000   JUVENILE FICTION / Action & Adventure / General
JUV002090   JUVENILE FICTION / Animals / Farm Animals
JUV030020   JUVENILE FICTION / People & Places / Asia
JUV025000   JUVENILE FICTION / Lifestyles / Farm & Ranch Life

ISBN 978-81-8190-312-9

Distributed in the United States by Consortium Book Sales & Distribution
www.cbsd.com